Serendipitous Hope

A Rory Odell Caribbean Adventure

By William Joseph Roberts

Black Anvil - Blue Rose Press
Chickamauga, GA USA

Table of Contents

Chapter 1

"Fire!" The captain leveled his longsword toward the pirate brig off to our port side. All eight cannons boomed, belching fire and smoke from the side of the ship.

"Hard to starboard!"

"Aye! Hard to starboard," the sailing master repeated from the foredeck of *Poseidon's Glory*, an English fluyt bound for Port Royal.

"Turn her, lads!" The captain grabbed the wheel, turning the ship hard to the right. "We might stand a chance against those cutthroats if we can bring her around for another volley! Ready the starboard cannons!"

Men hurried about the deck, reloading the guns and preparing to be boarded.

"Rory! Come here, boy," the captain shouted at me. "Fetch my brace of pistols from my cabin and make damn sure that they are all loaded!"

"Aye, Captain," I said with a quick salute before leaping down the stairs to the main deck. I'd learned early on after being captured by a press gang to do as ordered or the punishment would be severe. Nothing I had ever faced in my short eighteen years could have prepared me for how hard or exhausting life at sea could be.

Cannon fire roared behind me as I latched the door to the captain's cabin closed. Even behind the heavy timber walls, I could easily make out the shouted orders from above deck. The cabin was a complete disaster, even for the worst slob I'd ever had the misfortune to know. Chittering rats scurried away to the nooks and crannies of the cabin. A half-eaten moldy apple sat atop the chart table, swarmed by flies. Wading my way through the chaos, I found the captain's bracer of pistols hanging from the corner of his bunk. I quickly checked each of the five flintlocks then grabbed the powder horn and ammo pouch before I sprinted for the door.

The ship rocked beneath my feet and I found the deck coming up quickly to meet my face. Everything shook violently. The entire front wall of the cabin disintegrated into a shower of smoldering splinters. The cracking of wood popped and resounded as I watched the foremast collapse back onto the deck. Screams of painful agony overwhelmed the captain's shouted orders. A misty red cloud lingered about the exposed crew caught on deck by a volley of grapeshot. The unfortunate sailors slumped lifelessly to the deck.

"Strike our colors!" Someone on deck shouted.

"Belay that! Prepare to repel boarders," I heard the captain shout in reply.

I rushed out on deck and sprinted up the half-broken steps, delivering the captain's bracers as he'd ordered.

He draped the ammo pouch and powder horn over one shoulder and the bracer over the other. He sighed deeply then stepped toe to toe with me. I shuddered, but knew better than to pull away as he cupped the side of my face in his calloused palm. "You've been a good lad, and a more than worthwhile cabin boy. Stay low and don't do anything stupid. You should make it through this without a worry. I've no doubt they'll take you on when this is all over." He flashed a sad smile, then gently tapped me on the cheek. "Take care of yourself, lad." He nodded then turned, looking out over the stern railing, and obscenely motioned at the crew of the approaching ship.

The pursuing ships' bow guns fired, their rounds effortlessly tearing through the rear railing of the upper deck and the captain. His broken and mangled remains toppled to the main deck below. It happened so suddenly that I froze, staring at the shattered remains of my captor.

"Strike the bloody colors, and lower the sails!" the quartermaster, Mister Smyth bellowed. "You! Hoist the white flag!" He shoved the closest seaman toward the flag locker. "We've no choice but to surrender and hope they don't slit all our throats."

I watched as an injured and bleeding seaman lowered the Union Jack from the foremast and replaced it with a bone-white square of canvas.

In mere moments, the brig pulled alongside. Sailors tossed grappling hooks across the short distance, hooking into our ship's starboard railing.

The remaining crewmen gathered on the main deck, their hands empty and outstretched as sailors from the pirate brig poured over the railing and immediately ran below decks.

A large, blond-headed man leaped across the railing and landed heavily on the deck of *Poseidon's Glory*. "Who's the captain?"

"'The captain is dead," Mister Smyth announced, stepping forward toward the pirate captain. Two sailors stepped in front of the large pirate, shielding him from possible attack. The quartermaster stopped, sucking in a steadying breath. "What's left of the poor bastard is just over there," he said, pointing with a chin nod. "I'll be representing the crew."

"And you are?"

"Jonas Smyth, ship's quartermaster, sir," he said proudly, tucking his thumbs under his belt.

"Stand down," the pirate captain said as he pushed his men aside and stepped toward Mister Smyth. "I'm of no mind to tow a crippled ship to port. Will you and your men join with me, or would you rather take your chances on a sinking ship?"

Quiet grumbles and murmurs arose from the remaining crew before they nodded to Mister Smyth. "Looks as if we'll be joining your crew, sir," he said, turning back to the pirate captain.

"Good, good. I never did care much for unnecessary bloodshed." Removing his tricorn hat, he wiped away the sweat from his brow with the back of his hand. "Take everything of value on board and move as many of these cannons and rounds as we have tonnage for, Boots," he said, turning to an angry-looking seaman with a single bushy thick eyebrow.

"Aye! You heard the captain! Welcome aboard *Lucifer's Wrath*. Now get to loading," Boots shouted at what remained of our crew from *Poseidon's Glory*.

"Captain!" Another seaman shouted as he appeared from below deck. He led a large shackled negro man. "Looks as if we've stumbled upon a small fortune." He laughed, flashing a toothless smile. The captain looked the prisoner over, inspecting the man like livestock.

"Malnourished, but nonetheless I'd say a prize worthy of our time. Mister Smyth!"

"Aye, sir?"

"How many others are below?"

"Hundred and fifty-two at last count, sir. But that was also two days ago when we last fed them. Been a rough journey from the Barbary coast, sir. We started out with two hundred sixty, tons of fancy cloth, and a ton or so of household goods when we first set out. Between storms and illness, we've lost over half of the cargo we started with two months ago."

"How were you set on supplies, Mister Smyth?"

"As long as nothing was lost to spoilage, we should have a good two weeks left at least, sir. The captain had originally planned to put in at the Turks to resupply since we were limited on space for provisions. We managed to stretch that out a wee bit more with the loss of cargo over the course of the voyage."

"Then Mister Smyth, consider it your primary duty as a member of my crew to restore our prize to a sellable condition before we make port."

"Aye, sir. That I will," Mister Smyth said, stammering. "And how long would I have to do that, sir?"

"I aim to make for Nassau to resupply, then on to Charleston Harbor where we'll fetch the best price for our bounty."

"Aye, that I have no doubt, sir." Mister Smyth nodded then turned, leading the prisoner by his shackles to *Lucifer's Wrath*.

"Captain!"

All eyes snapped upward to a man standing atop the mainsail boom. Even from this distance, he radiated a roguish charm that I'd not encountered in any other seamen. His thick black shoulder-length curls fluttered in the warm tradewinds. The dashing rogue lowered himself from the boom to the deck of our doomed fluyt, landing with a loud thump of his hard-soled boots. All work on deck stopped as crewmen gathered, circling around the Captain and this rogue.

"Wouldn't we fare far better if those men were free and added to the rosters?" His tone was smooth, almost sultry, and heavily accented with a French flavor. "Extra hands never go amiss when boarding a prized target, Captain."

Nodded heads and muttered '*Ayes*' answered the rogue's question from all around the gathered crew.

The captain chuckled. "You are as persistent as a boil, aren't you? And how would you suggest that we should creep our way near enough to one of your mythical treasure ships in order to board her, Mister Bouchard? We'd be cut to pieces by forty guns or more before we could ever hope to get close."

"Not if you know where they will be when their guard is at its lowest, Captain." Mister Bouchard strutted slowly about in front of the captain.

"This is neither the time nor the place, crewman. We've work to do before our luck runs out and we're spotted. Need I remind you that we are in English waters and they do not look kindly on piratical actions against the ships of their countrymen."

"That is something that I think we can all agree upon, Captain," Mister Bouchard said, throwing his arms above his head with a flourish. "Am I right, lads?"

The crew roared with cheers and *'Ayes'*.

"But I see no need in breaking our own backs moving the goods and guns when we've a hundred and fifty-two extra sets of hands to divide the work."

The sound of a pistol sliding free of a leather holster drew everyone's attention toward Boots, the *Wrath's* quartermaster. In what seemed like less than the span of a heartbeat, Boots had a cocked flintlock pointed at Bouchard's head.

"You'll do as the captain ordered or you'll find yourself swimming deep to meet Old Hob himself."

The gathered crew surrounded Boots, blocking his shot. One of the sailors motioned for the pistol and disarmed the quartermaster without a fight.

"Mutiny is it?"

I could see the captain's jaw angrily flex from where I stood on the poop deck. His eyes darted back and forth, examining the gathered crew as he calculated his next move.

"Be sensible, Captain. I think the crew has already decided our next step for you," Bouchard proudly stated in a knowing tone.

The pirate captain's hand lept for the pistol secured in his belt. He had barely gripped the weapon's polished wooden shaft before fire and smoke roiled from the end of Bouchard's own pistol.

"My regards to Old Hob," Bouchard said with a smile and a flourished salute.

The captain collapsed to his knees then fell over face first with a loud thud. Blood poured out onto the deck from the wound in the dead captain's head.

"What say you, lads?"

Bouchard jumped atop the port side railing, holding himself steady against the Jacob's ladder that rose to meet the mainmast.

"Shouldn't we free these unlucky bastards and give them the same fighting chance at a better life that we've had?"

The crew erupted in shouts and cheers.

"Then I think that's been decided." Bouchard let out a long whooping shout. "You, sir," he shouted, pointing into the crowd. "Mister Smyth was it?"

"Aye, sir. That be my name."

"Then see to it that these men are fed well and added to our rosters."

Mister Smyth nodded, "Aye sir, easy enough."

"You and you," Bouchard said, pointing at two of the seamen restraining Boots. "I'm not a cold-hearted man by any means, but I'm unsure what I should do with him for the moment. Take him below and lock him away for now. We can decide what to do with him after we make landfall. As for the rest of you, transfer the cargo and as many of the guns as possible. Restock our powder and munitions, then make ready to sail with both ships. We'll tow her if we must, but I'd prefer she sail as much under her own power as possible. Cut away the broken mast and rigging if need be. She may be damaged, but she'll still fetch a fair price in port."

The crew hurried to work, forming lines to pass cases of goods and supplies across to the pirate brig. The newly freed men joined the lines, grateful to be relieved of their restraints and above deck in the fresh sea air.

That's when Bouchard happened to glance over and notice me staring down at him and the commotion on the main deck. Bouchard smiled wide then sauntered in my direction.

"What is your name, boy?" A hint of interest glistened in his eyes.

"R...Rory, sir. Rory Odell," I said, stumbling over my own name.

"Rory," he said, gently rolling the r's. "You look to be an able lad. Why are you not below? You do not look like you are injured?"

"No sir, I'm not."

"What is your position, crewman?"

"Cabin boy, sir."

"Then what keeps you from your duties, lad?" He crossed his arms over his chest, then began twirling the tip of his curly waxed mustache between his thumb and forefinger.

"N...Nothing, sir. Right away, sir."

He grabbed me forcefully by the upper arm, stopping me in my tracks.

"Clear the captain's quarters if you please, Mister Odell, and deliver his effects to my new cabin aboard the *Wrath*.

He stared me directly in the eyes so intently, I'd have thought he was trying to examine my very soul.

"Aye aye, sir." I hurried away down the broken steps and back into the captain's cabin.

Chapter 2

With the extra hands, we'd finished transferring all cargo and making repairs in short order before setting sail once again. The crew of *Poseidon's Glory* continued aboard her as if nothing had happened, with Mister Smyth in charge as acting captain. The freedmen eagerly went to work, glad to be free of the shackles and lower decks of the ship. They were divided between both ships and put to work with others or assigned menial tasks that required no real training.

We sailed northeast for days with no sign of land in sight. As the ship's stores grew shorter, the crew grew restless, claiming Mister Bouchard was the devil himself, and that he was leading us straight for the maw of hell hidden somewhere in the depths of the Sargasso sea. Mister Smyth warned me that talk of mutiny and turning the ship for the nearest English port were on the rise. He didn't want me caught in the middle of a conflict that was sure to end in bloodshed.

"Land Ho!" cried the lookout, stationed high in the crow's nest atop the mainmast.

Mister Smyth was as surprised as any other knowledgeable sailor aboard. No one with any sense about them sailed this far out for any reason other than to hide or circumvent a meeting at sea. But there it was. A lush green tropical island in the middle of nowhere. From this distance, it looked to be a few miles wide with tall peaks rising hundreds of feet above sea level. Mister Smyth told me that he couldn't find the island on any of the maps that we had onboard, but reminded me that maps can always be outdated or wrong.

We sailed into the protected harbor of a beautiful green bay, following close behind *Lucifer's Wrath*. The bay's waters were deep and almost glowing in the dimming light of evening. Pulling in alongside *Lucifer's Wrath* and dropping anchor we went to work securing the ships together on the captain's orders.

Crowds of people gathered along the shore as dozens of small boats set off in our direction. To my surprise, each of them was manned by a mixture of men and women from many nations.

Most looked to be natives of the new world to me. They were short, with a dark golden brown skin tone and straight raven black hair worn long or cut in what amounted to a bowl cut. They adorned themselves with jewelry of bone and shells, along with wooden rings worn in their elongated earlobes. Black tribal tattoos covered most of their bodies, especially their faces. The rest of the population looked to be made up primarily of Africans, while a few were of European or East Indian descent. That in itself was nothing out of the ordinary I suppose. Most ports of call had a mixture of people from all over. The shocking and more than distracting part of their arrival was the fact that most were nude or nearly nude. Most of the natives, both men and women wore what amounted to little more than a leather thong around their waist. It was all strange and intoxicating, to say the least. Never in my years had I imagined a setting and its people as beautiful and exotic as this.

With the aid of the islanders, we unloaded both ships in the span of a few hours, setting up camp along the beach.

As acting captain of *Poseidon's Glory*, Mister Smyth retained me in his employ as the ship's cabin boy and put me to work setting up our tent.

"Mister Smyth!"

I turned to see Captain Bouchard approaching with a small native woman following along beside him.

"Aye, Captain. What can I do for you, sir?" Mister Smyth turned, looking up from where he knelt, preparing a cookfire.

Bouchard eyed the encampment and smiled, thrusting his thumbs under his belt.

"If you'd be so kind as to come with me. We should visit the chief before the hour becomes any later. Necahual here will attend to your camp and complete its setup," he said, motioning toward the young native girl.

"Oh, aye," Mister Smyth said with an agreeing nod. "Gladly, sir. But I'm not sure why you need me to attend the chief with you."

"Because you represent the second ship, Mister Smyth." Bouchard flashed a tired look in the quartermaster's direction. "I spent quite some time among these people not so long ago, and I myself am a welcome guest. But the fact is that I have brought hundreds of mouths to their limited shores without warning or reason. It is my opinion that we must go and explain ourselves before our welcome has been worn out."

Mister Smyth furrowed his brow in thought. "I still don't understand why you need me, sir."

Bouchard let out an exasperated huff. "I intend to request sanctuary for those who would wish it, Mister Smyth. You will be my witness to the conditions those men and women were forced to suffer in the belly of your holds. Then I intend to establish a safe haven of my own on these shores from which to operate. But that is only if I can convince the chief to allow us to stay. Should he refuse, we will need to be off at first light for the closest port."

Mister Smyth stood, dropping the bundle of sticks he had been preparing for the fire, and dusted his hands. "Ready whenever you are, sir."

Necahual knelt and continued to prepare the cook fire that the quartermaster had started.

"Then let's be off," Bouchard said as he started to walk away, then stopped and turned, looking back at me. "Why don't you come along with us, Mister Odell? I have a feeling it would be a worthwhile experience for you. It can only aid in your education of diplomacy and negotiations."

The corners of his mouth quirked with a mischievous smile, painting his expression with a look of calculated interest.

I turned away as I felt the color rise in my cheeks. I could feel a knot of anxiety forming in my chest.

No one had ever looked at me like that before. Growing up on the streets of Dublin, people only saw me as a thing to be ignored. A filthy ragamuffin that one should keep a wary eye on and stay at a distance as they passed by. The previous captain of *Poseidon's Glory* was somewhat better than that. Even though his men kidnapped me and pressed me into service, he didn't treat me like the other slaves on board. He was by no means a gentleman, though he did treat me kindly when in the right mood.

Unsure of what I should say, I remained silent. I dared not refuse his request, he was the captain after all, and could just as easily have me strung up from the yardarm as to invite me to dine at his table.

"Come lad, let us not dawdle," Bouchard said as he returned to my side and draped his arm over my shoulders. "Any new encounter can be looked upon as a worthwhile experience, my boy. You may find a silver lining, even though you may not see it at the time."

Chapter 3

The meeting with the chief of the Saragosans was an odd one, to say the least. Spoken in a broken mixture of French, African, and their native tongue that resembled a sing-song melody at times where its rhythm was broken only by the odd-sounding word of French or Portuguese thrown in.

Captain Bouchard first negotiated with the chief for sanctuary of the African slaves. Explaining that no man should be forced to do the bidding of another and that he at least had partial knowledge of the life of a slave as he'd had his own first-hand experience. He'd explained that at one time he too had been pressed into service at a young age as I had. During the discussion he'd pointed at me, using me as a visual reference I assumed.

He continued to explain how, if allowed, those who wished to remain on the island could aid in fishing and farming, adding to the quality of life of the Saragosan people. He continued to say that for those who did not wish to stay, he would employ them as crew to either serve aboard one of the ships or establish his own small farmstead. At the least, he would deliver any man who wished to leave to the next port of call, whenever and wherever that may be.

In the end, his overall intention was to repay the kindness shown to him by the Saragosan people so many years ago when he'd found himself shipwrecked upon the island's shores. He promised to bring goods and supplies to Port Lambert and that he would eagerly export any goods they wished.

The chief's primary concern was that allowing so many others to know of their whereabouts, could lead to disaster.

After a great deal of deliberation, the hold of bolt cloth and household goods was given to the chief and his people as a gift, and many more promises were made on Captain Bouchard's part. The chief reluctantly agreed to the terms offered, but only for the term of a year and a day, where the agreement would be reevaluated for another year. If at any time Bouchard or his men failed to abide by the accord, then they must immediately depart and never return to the shores of Saragasso.

We followed behind Captain Bouchard as he departed the chief's long hut. Pleased with himself, he grinned ear to ear and discussed plans with Mister Smyth as we made our way back to the encampment.

The next day camp was struck at the captain's order and moved with haste to the far side of the bay.

Before Mister Smyth and I had finished setting up our shelter, Necahual, Captain Bouchard's assistant, approached. She pointed toward me and said something in her native tongue then motioned for me to follow.

Unsure what to do I looked to Mister Smyth.

"Did you catch any of that, Mister Smyth?"

"No, but it's probably best to go with her, lad," Mister Smyth said in a fatherly tone. "Most likely the captain has summoned you for an errand or some such thing."

"What about our shelter?"

"Nothing to worry yourself over lad. I'll manage perfectly fine till you get back."

Slapping me on the shoulder, he smiled then turned back to the work at hand.

Following Necahual, I couldn't help but think that the captain could only want one thing from me considering how he nearly leered at me the night before. If we could only make port I could escape and maybe even make my way home back to Ireland.

The native woman led me through the jungle where others were clearing underbrush and making space to build upon. After a short climb up a small hillside, we arrived at a fully established encampment on the eastern face of the island. Leading me to a large campaign tent in the middle of the hillside encampment, she held open the door flap motioning me inside.

I removed my headwrap as I ducked through the opening.

"Oh, ah ha! Mister Odell," Captain Bouchard said in his exaggerated French accent. "Thank you for coming so quickly. Please, sit," he said, motioning toward a stack of crates to the left of the tent flap.

Dusting out two brass mugs, Captain Bouchard pulled the cork from a clear glass bottle with his teeth, then poured a bit of drink into each of the mugs.

Setting down the bottle he recorked it, handing me one of the mugs.

"I'm sure that you're curious as to why I called you to my tent." He quirked a smile then took a quick contemplative sip.

"I plan to sail my way across the Caribbean to fame and glory, but to do so, I will need an assistant that I can emphatically trust with my life."

He took another sip then sat and leaned back on a pile of sacks stacked to resemble a chair of sorts.

"I need someone I can count on, Mister Odell. Someone who will keep my best interests in mind and keep my secrets away from those who would do me harm."

"But what about Mister Smyth, sir? Wouldn't he be more suited for the task?"

"Oh, he would indeed, but he and his skill are required to operate *Posidon's Glory*."

He took another sip of rum then set his mug aside and leaned forward, steepling his fingers over his face in thought.

"I would like for you to continue your duties as ship's cabin boy, Rory. May I call you Rory?"

Just as I had feared. He was no different than the previous captain. Nothing would change. Better to die a free man than to be forced to lick another man's boots.

"No, you may not, sir. And while I haven't a problem in carrying out my duties to earn my keep, I refuse to be a slave to any man. Nor will I idly allow myself to be another man's whore. If you've a need, sir, then find another or tend to it yourself!"

Startled at the words that spewed from my lips unabated, I shifted nervously. I glanced about, taking account of my surroundings, unsure of what the captain's response would be.

He stared at me, his mouth downturned in an angry scowl that grew deeper as the moments passed, then suddenly Captain Bouchard burst out into hysterical laughter.

"I take it that short of shackles and a leash, you'll not change your mind then?" He chuckled, then took another sip of his rum.

"Laugh all you want, but I'm serious, Captain."

"I'm sure that you are, Rory, and as amusing as this is, if you are quite done flexing your will, may we move on to more productive discussions? You along with every other member of this crew are free men, Mister Odell."

The curled tips of his waxed mustache bounced as he flashed a knowing smile, then emptied his mug.

"My aim, my dear boy, is to make for Tortuga with a full crew aboard *Lucifer's Wrath* and *Posidon's Glory* in tow. We'll leave the men who wish to be free there to make their own way in the world, sell the *Glory,* and visit the governor where I hope to acquire a Letter of Marque. From there we'll provision and repair the *Wrath.*" He flashed another smile and laughed. "What say you, crewman? Wish to be the right hand of an unknown scallywag, bound to make his fame and fortune on the high seas of the Caribbean?"

Chapter 4

"Sail on the Horizon!"

It had only been three days after setting out from Port Lambert when I'd spotted a sail peeking over the swells to the north of us. Before sending me up the mast for watch duty, Captain Bouchard mentioned that we should be just south of the Grand Turks. If that was true, the ship in the distance was most likely English.

Raising the spyglass to the north, I could make out that the ship had three square-rigged masts. Banners of blue and red fluttered in the stiff southwestern breeze.

"What can you make out, Mister Odell?"

I looked down to see Captain Bouchard staring up at me from the poop deck.

"Three masts, square-rigged. She's flying banners of blue and red. I can't quite make out her flag yet."

"In these waters, she's most likely an English patrol. No doubt they'll be wanting to inspect our cargo and impose a tax of some sort."

He smiled wide, then looked about at the men. "Well, what are you all waiting for? Prepare this ship for battle."

"Sir?" I heard the sailing master ask from somewhere on the foredeck.

"You heard me. Make ready for battle, gentlemen! And loosen those sails a bit. Let them think we are inept and sloppy."

I leaned over the rail of the small crow's nest probably farther than I should, looking down at the captain. "And what is your plan, if I may ask, my Captain?"

He glanced up and smiled. "I mean to board that ship and liberate the contents of its hold, thereby depriving King George of the taxes he would have otherwise received."

He turned to Daniel Curtis, the new quartermaster of *Lucifer's Wrath*, following the removal of Boots from the position. "Load the guns with grapeshot and ready the falconets. Do it quickly before they are close enough to see what we are about. We'll pose as a merchant ship aiding the crew of *Poseidon's Glory*. If they follow procedure, they'll pull alongside and board us. Most of their men will be on deck preparing for an inspection and that's when we'll catch them unawares."

"Aye, sir! You dogs heard the captain! Heave to and ready the guns!" Mister Curtis rushed below into the cargo hold.

As the distant ship approached it did indeed reveal itself to be of English origins, and a corvette no less. Regardless, Captain Bouchard's mind was set. He desperately wanted that ship and its cargo. There was a glimmer of desire in his eyes as he looked out across the water.

In preparation for the upcoming battle, he ordered me from the lookout and armed me with one of his own beautifully engraved flintlock pistols. Silver and bronze plating ever so delicately etched covered the blue steel barrel and the dark hardwood of the weapon. It was a work of art as much as it was a weapon of war. The image of a mermaid stood out along the silvered side plate, just as it did on the duplicate weapon tucked into Captain Bouchard's belt.

He then handed me a sword in its scabbard and bid me to belt it on. Doing so I drew the long curved blade from its scabbard and admired the craftsmanship.

"The coming fight will in no way be an easy one. I hope you know how to use that."

"You swing and stab with it. Nothing so hard about that."

Captain Bouchard let out an exasperated chuckle then took a step back. Crossing his arms he tapped a finger to his lips as he examined me.

"Let me see your stance. Attack the mast like it were a filthy English dog about to take your life."

Doing as ordered I swung the blade sideways, chipping away a small sliver of wood from the mast.

"Oh, my boy, that will not do at all. It is a pity that we do not have time to properly train you."

"What did I do wrong?"

Clicking his tongue with a disapproving tisk, the captain's thick black curls swayed with the shake of his head.

"You're too stiff and your stance is all wrong. If you stand straight up and down like that you make yourself a very easy target to hit. But if you turn sideways, staggering your stance, you will make for a smaller target and therefore far harder to hit if your defense is worth a damn. Here, let me show you," he said, drawing his own long sword from its scabbard.

Stepping to his left, he gracefully slipped his right foot behind and to the side followed by his left, nearly dancing as he rounded the mast and lunged at me.

"Do you see how my profile is narrower if I turn to the side like this, instead of facing straight on with you?"

"I think so," I said as I turned sideways, spreading my stance.

"Good, that looks promising." Captain Bouchard twisted the waxed tip of his mustache. "Continue practicing. We have a few moments before the English arrive to impose their will upon us."

In less than an hour, the English ship had fired a warning shot from one of its bow cannons to get our attention. The English commander must have been livid by that point because they were close enough that we could make out the individuals on deck. Someone, possibly the first mate, held up a large cone and shouted orders to lower the sails across the distance to us. He and another in the blue coats of the royal navy stood on the foredeck of the English corvette, spyglass in hand.

Just as Captain Bouchard had predicted, the English ordered us to stand to as they came along our port side. The English sailors in their pristine crewman uniforms went about their duties as instructed to the letter.

A number of the English crewmen tossed hooks across the distance that our crew gathered, securing the lines to mooring cleats along the side rail.

"How fares your day, mon ami? Well, I would hope," Captain Bouchard said, bowing deeply with a flourish of his hat to the English captain who stood stoically along the railing of his beautifully ornate corvette.

The English captain scoffed. "I am in no way your friend, sir," he said with a growl. "You will address me as Lieutenant Commander Harding."

"As you wish, Lieutenant Commander," Captain Bouchard replied with a slight bow of the head.

The English sailors pulled on the ropes, slowly drawing the ships together and closing the gap.

"Please dispense with the formalities, sir. Are your records and cargo prepared for inspection? I have no wish to dawdle about on this pathetic excuse for a ship." As if to add insult to injury, Commander Harding produced a handkerchief from his pocket and covered his nose.

"As you wish." Captain Bouchard crossed his arms and laughed. "I'd be more than happy to show you what we have to offer, Commander."

"Lieutenant Commander," the English Captain shouted.

"Mister Curtis, if you would please."

"Aye, sir!"

Mister Curtis blew a shrill warbled chime on a bosun's whistle. Men suddenly flooded from below decks and ran out the guns while a number of crewmen appeared from the aft cabin with a burning taper in hand. In moments each of the *Wrath's* eight guns fired their salvo at the English corvette.

Men all across the corvette's deck fell in the bloody massacre, shredded by the nearly point-blank eight-gun salute from our Brigantine.

Hooks flew across the distance to the English ship, grappling the other ship's railing.

"Prepare to board her!"

The two falconets boomed from the aft deck as sailors fired upon the English crew emerging from below decks.

It was truly a strange sight to witness. A mixture of missiles pummeled the English crewmen. From Flintlock pistols and rifles to longbows and spears, the deadly projectiles soared across the distance, finding their mark.

As the ships crashed together, Captain Bouchard valiantly led the charge onto the English ship. Leaping across the distance he drew his sword, cutting a deep gash across the chest of the first man he encountered.

Following close behind I drew my own sword, lunging for a man that came at the captain from his right.

The sailor blocked my attack, easily batting it away then came back around, knocking the blade from my grip.

I drew the pistol from my waistband, cocked, aimed, and fired. The sailor flinched as the round grazed his neck.

Patting at the bloody wound, he scowled then roared, charging straight at me, his sword held high.

Backing up I stumbled and tripped over something lying on the deck behind me. Landing with a hard thud atop the still-warm body of an English sailor I coughed, trying to regain my breath.

The seaman that I'd shot raised his blade, poised to plunge the weapon deep into me when the point of another long narrow blade suddenly appeared from his chest.

Falling to his knees the sailor grasped at the blade, staring at it with a confused look. Unable to comprehend what had just happened to him before he slumped forward, falling face first to the wooden deck.

Captain Bouchard wiped the blade of his longsword on the dead man's back.

"Carelessness does not become you, Mister Odell." The captain smiled then sheathing his sword, he held out a hand in my direction.

"Come, let us see what spoils of war we have earned."

Chapter 5

Spoils of war indeed. Captain Bouchard insisted that I come along with him to inspect the captain's cabin after the battle. According to the ship's logs, the *Sea Nymph*, as the English corvette was called, had been out on patrol in the waters surrounding the Grand Turks, stopping all merchant ships and charging them a protection tax. In essence, the previous captain had misused his authority and strong-armed hard-working crews out of their cargo at the threat of meeting Davy Jones if they didn't comply with his orders.

Earlier in the week, he'd ordered the sinking of two Spanish sloops bound for Santo Domingo when they refused to come to and be boarded. According to his personal logs, he was surprised to find a very wealthy Spanish nobleman floating among the wreckage, whom they promptly took aboard and placed in chains below.

Besides a prisoner, with which to ransom and a handsome new ship, we'd also gained fifteen tons of mixed cargo in the form of tobacco, spices, cotton, sugar, and a number of casks of rum.

Pleased with this finding, Captain Bouchard ordered a ration to each man for the swift battle and our fine prize.

We continued on our course and arrived in the bustling port of Tortuga just over three days later.

"Rory!" The captain bellowed from within his cabin.

I rushed through the bustle of men working on the main deck, preparing the ship to pull into port. When I entered the captain's quarters I found him relaxing with his feet up on the chart table. Captain Bouchard twirled a very ornate felt hat on the tip of his finger. It was a deep shade of red, with a wide brim that was tacked up on the left side. A multitude of feathers decorating its band danced and fluttered as it spun,

"I have come to the conclusion that the previous captain of this ship was flamboyantly closeted due to the number of fine articles of clothing I have found squirreled away within his personal wardrobe and sea chests."

"If you pardon my asking sir, what does that have to do with me?"

"After finding such finery, I began thinking that first impressions are a must, are they not? Would you have ever guessed that the Lieutenant Commander owned let alone wore anything not issued by the Royal Navy?"

"No, sir. He looked like any other career officer to me."

"And that's exactly my point." Captain Bouchard swung his feet from the table and stood in one swift motion, gliding across the deck to stand before me. "Which means that we must look our very best and present the personas with which we wish the governor of Tortuga to witness."

He smiled wide, placing the wide-brimmed feathered hat atop my head.

"The color does not suit you, but the style does accentuate your features marvelously."

I jerked back away from him. "I'll not be…"

"Yes, yes. I know. You'll not be any man's whore," he drolled with a roll of his eyes.

"No, I was going to say doxie, but whore works as well."

"You mistake my intent, sir. I do not want you for my whore, Mister Odell, but I do require your assistance. I mean to visit the governor and in doing so, I must make a good first impression. A man of wealth and position can respect another of similar status. I suspect to come away with the best possible outcome that we should play the parts of a wealthy nobleman and his escort."

He smiled, laughing at a thought. "What we have here will not do, though there are boots, belts, and the like that will suit us fine. But to look the part we must go see an old friend of mine."

"And who might this friend be?"

"Mister Brendan Smith, a tailor of the highest quality for finery and attire this side of the Atlantic. That's if he and his shop are still in Tortuga. It has been a number of years since I last visited there. But we shall see once we drop anchor and go ashore. What say you? Care to let me dress you up in some of the new world's greatest finery?"

I really didn't have any prospects besides begging in the streets of Tortuga, so reluctantly I agreed to the captain's request. Better the devil you know and I at least had Mister Smyth watching my back.

No sooner had the anchor dropped in the harbor than the captain and I were aboard a longboat rowing for shore. The quartermasters, Mister Smyth, and Mister Curtis were left in charge of the ships and ordered to sell all of the cargo.

After transferring additional guns and ammunition to the *Sea Nymph*, they were ordered to fill the magazine aboard the corvette. While the captain and I attended to his plan, they would reprovision and reconfigure the corvette, adding additional gun ports along both sides and installing both bow and stern chasers to her compliment. Once completed, they were ordered to get the best price possible for both the brigantine and the fluyt before issuing pay to the men.

Turning a corner from the main thoroughfare that ran from the seaside docks to the town gates, we made our way down a narrow side street. Wooden signs hung above a number of doorways along the littered and urine-soaked street.

"Even though his shingle still hangs above the door, I fear that things are no longer as prosperous as they once were for my old friend," the captain said, pressing a silky white handkerchief to his nose. "Come, open the door. Let us hope the stink only lingers without."

"Aye, captain," I said. A small bell chimed as I pushed open the shop door.

Bolts of fine silks, richly colored cloth, and other raw materials lined shelves along the back wall of the shop. Dresses, complete with petticoats, corsets, and matching sun bonnets fit for any lady of high standing hung from dummy forms throughout the shop, displaying their exquisite finery.

"One moment," an older-sounding gentleman announced from an unseen alcove. "Please, have a look around while you wait, I will be out momentarily."

Captain Bouchard turned to me and smiled. "We are very fortunate," he said with a nod then leaned in close, whispering. "I have no doubt that my old friend will have something hidden away to suit our needs. He is as sly as a fox in that regard. He will display his wares and present you with the finest of garments. Then just as you should wish to take your leave, he will produce an article that you did not even realize that you wanted in the first place, making it extremely hard to refuse."

Shuffling feet preceded the appearance of a white-haired gentleman in ornately embroidered trousers and vest over a finely spun silk shirt and stockings. Removing a small pair of spectacles from his nose, he polished the small lenses with a handkerchief then placed them atop his head and smacked his hands together, rubbing them vigorously.

"Now, how may I be of service to you two fine gentlemen?"

Captain Bouchard tipped his chin upward, looking down the bridge of his nose at the aged tailor.

"I was informed that you carried the finest of wares in the city, my dear tailor," he said with a wrinkle of his nose. "But if the stench of your doorstep is any indication, then I fear I may be wasting my time."

"Oh no, M'lord. You have not," Mister Smith said confidently. "Even though the sots and beggars tend to linger about late at night, it is in no way a reflection on the quality of my work, sir."

Captain Bouchard smiled at the tailor then glanced over to me with a mischievous grin. "Very well then, my dear Mister Smith. My companion and I require something appropriate and presentable for a clandestine meeting with the governor. If you guarantee your quality, then let's see what you have to offer, if you would please. Bring out your best.

I sipped at a sweet, but tart and very alcoholic wine that the tailor had provided us with while we waited. Immediately taking our measurements, he rushed about the shop, producing complete outfits seemingly from thin air that were roughly in our sizes. After a brief inspection, Captain Bouchard selected a lightweight jacket and trousers for himself which was accented with panels of embroidered red silk, and another similarly styled outfit trimmed in a light blue for myself. After a brief fitting and double-check of measurements, the tailor escorted us to a very posh waiting room off to the side of the shop's main room.

The captain lounged in a thickly cushioned armchair with his feet propped on a similarly upholstered ottoman. He swirled the chilled wine in his glass, inhaled deeply, then sipped at its sweetness. I paced about the room, inspecting this or that odd trinket or painting that decorated the ornate chamber. The awkward silence as we waited was almost deafening. It was strangely amplified by the ticking of a great grandfather clock in the corner of the room and occasionally broken by the clatter of the tailor's efforts in another room.

"Please," Captain Bouchard said, motioning to the armchair across from him. "Do sit and speak with me before the silence drives me to insanity. As it stands my sanity balances on the thin edge of going quite mad."

I turned back to the cat curio I had been examining before he spoke and picked it up, turning it over in my grasp.

"What would you like to speak about?"

"I'm curious," he said. He propped his head against his hand, his forefinger tapping at his temple.

"Curious about?" I returned the curio to its place atop the mantle and continued along, inspecting the other uninteresting items that decorated its aged surface.

He swirled his wine and sipped at it once again. "I am absolutely curious about you, Mister Odell."

"How so?" I glanced over at him and then back to a painting of tropical fruit that hung on the far wall. "I am nothing more than an uninteresting man in an uninteresting occupation."

"On a ship full of cutthroats and scallywags," Bouchard added.

"That is true. Which does add an element of stress and the unknown to my daily expectations, but all in all, Rory Odell is nothing more than an uninteresting individual."

"Then please, if you would, Mister Odell," he said, motioning to the armchair. "Indulge me."

"Very well, as you wish, Captain."

After refilling both of our glasses, I took the indicated seat.

"What would you like to know, Captain?"

"Please, Rory. *Captain* is entirely too formal. Call me Louis." He shifted, placing one foot on the ground then crossing his leg as he wiggled deep into the armchair's plush cushions.

"Very well, Louis," I said, nodding. "What is it that you would like to know?"

Louis flashed a perturbed smile, then swirled his wine once again. "My, you are gruff and direct, aren't you?"

"Just the way it is I suppose."

"Regardless of your lack of diplomatic finesse or polite social decorum, you fascinate me, Rory."

I opened my mouth to speak, but before I could, Louis interrupted me.

"Yes, yes, I do wish you would let me finish before you jump to conclusions, my dear boy. But that right there is precisely what intrigues me so much."

"What?"

"The thing that has caused you to react in such a way as you do at any time you may suspect something is amiss."

He paused my next words with a single finger held aloft as he swirled his wine in contemplative thought, then sipped at the sweet red liquid.

"I see how you are with the crew and those whom you've encountered onshore. People love you, Rory. It is seemingly nothing for you to secure even the most fleeting of friendships in the blink of an eye, nor to maintain an enemy as such for long. You possess a gift that men like myself struggle to achieve every day of our lives. You have a kind and gentle heart that you wear on your sleeve, on display for all to see, but yet your wounds are as plain as the nose on your face."

"I don't believe I understand your meaning." I uncomfortably shifted in my seat and sipped at my own glass of wine.

Louis leaned forward, cupping the stem of the fine glass snifter between his laced fingers.

"In your interactions with the crew, I have observed even the slightest of suggestion being obeyed as if you had given an order, regardless of any conceived form of rank. But if someone pokes just the right spot, your demeanor shifts. It is a tell if nothing else, but it is there no matter how you attempt to hide it. Just as now for example. I'd wager that by the heavy flexing of your jaw muscles, that your teeth will be aching something awful by morning."

I froze, catching myself chewing on my own angry thoughts just as he had said.

"Your point, if you please, Captain."

"No man cares to be cornered, whether it be physically or metaphorically. But when a wounded animal feels cornered, it lashes out, flinches, gives away its tell, you see."

"Your point?"

"Who hurt you, Rory?" He asked in a soft and sincere tone.

"I don't see where that is any of your business," I said in a tone angrier than I thought possible.

"Do not wrongly construe my intent. You are a good man, Rory Odell, with a very promising career ahead of you. I only wish to help you heal and to move beyond the injury."

He leaned back and let out a long sigh, adjusting himself in the plush armchair. He sipped gingerly at his wine.

My mind raced with dredged-up memories of Dublin, surviving by God's own graces and the skills I had learned on the cold, unforgiving streets of that city as a child. Memories of my capture and forced servitude. Then, the freshest memories of all involving the captain of *Poseidon's Glory* raced through my mind.

"Please. Explain it to me, Rory. I want to understand."

I shuddered. An icy chill surged through me, invoked by a single escaping tear that ran down my cheek. My breath caught in my throat as I started to speak. Suddenly hoarse, I swallowed down the pain and bile that the memories had brought up to the surface of my mind.

"It's quite alright if you aren't ready to speak of it. But if you are, it is in complete confidence. Nothing goes beyond the walls of this room."

I suddenly found my soul overriding my stubborn pride and spilling all of its hurtful secrets to this man. To this all but utter stranger. For whatever reason, his words felt sincere and for once in my life, I felt safe.

I told him of my early childhood on the streets of Dublin. How I'd been left to fend for myself on the streets after my Da' had been murdered and I'd been placed in an orphanage by the authorities. The prospect of starvation outweighed the nightly beatings and other atrocities endured by the children in that wretched hole. I survived by whatever means I had to, but it was by my own choice.

There were many instances, too numerous to count, that I was not in the least proud of. But I did it to survive. And then, there were times when it wasn't for myself. There was a small crew of us running the streets for a number of years. We each looked out for one another and became a family of sorts over that short time.

That was at least before the press gangs began snatching up any able-bodied individual that no respectable person would miss or care about. Then my family began to slowly dwindle away until it was my turn. One night I was on the streets of Dublin, rolling dice and managing bets, the next, I was in the hold of a ship well out of sight of land.

At first, I was ordered to carry out menial work about *Posidon's Glory* or be faced with pain, or even worse, to be tossed overboard and left to feed the creatures of the deep. That was at least until the captain had taken notice of me.

Louis was left speechless. His face contorted with what looked like a mixture of anger and confusion when I explained how an act, when carried out willingly, was a vastly contrasting experience to one carried out at the end of a cocked pistol.

Louis quietly wept with me as we silently sipped our warming wine.

Chapter 6

By early afternoon, we had been forced to dress, undress, and redress a multitude of times at the prodding tip of the tailor's pins after what quite possibly could have been considered a nip too much of wine. After finding the bottom of our second bottle, we had both lost all sense of control and reverted to something akin to giggling school girls, merely laughing at nothing.

Dressed in our newly acquired finery, we rented a carriage and began the long slog uphill to the governor's estate which occupied a large portion of the hilltop near Fort de Rocher.

Paving stones and cultivated rows of fruit trees lined the wide roadway that winded slowly around the tropical hillside.

The carriage rumbled to a hasty stop at the bottom of a grand brick staircase leading up to the main entrance.

"I'm terribly sorry about that, sir," the driver said as he opened the carriage door. "Hope I didn't toss the two of you gentlemen about too much. This new filly can be a bit touchy at times. Not quite broken in all the way, you see."

"That is quite alright. There's been no harm done to either of our persons," Louis said with a nonchalant wave of the hand.

"You're too kind, sir." The driver bowed, holding the door open as we exited the carriage. "Would you like for me to wait, m'lord?"

Louis looked to me then back to the driver. "I believe so, sir. If the governor is available, our business should be brief. Water the horse and we'll send for you when we are ready to return to town." Louis held out his hand to the man who promptly took the offered bit of what looked like silver.

"Yes, m'lord," he said, nodding, then climbed back into the seat.

I examined the massive manor house and the elaborate gardens that filled the surrounding grounds. Beautiful flowers decorated the landscape, filling the air with their sweet fragrance.

The front door of the manor house opened. "May I help you, gentlemen?"

"We wish to speak with the governor on a matter of grave importance involving French pride and the sinking of Spanish ships," Louis said.

"Of course you do sir," the butler said. "And whom may I say is requesting an audience with his lordship?"

"Louis Bouchard, captain of the *Sea Nymph*, a twenty-gun corvette, at your service," he said, bowing low with a flourish of his feathered hat,

The butler stared down the length of his nose at us, unmoved by Louis's display.

"Indeed," the butler said, "if you will please follow me. You may wait in the sitting room whilst I announce your arrival to Lord d'Ogéron."

"Shall we?" Louis motioned toward the door.

"Thank you, kind sir," I said, nodding a bow to Louis as I followed my feet on the heels of the butler.

The house was a flurry of activity. Servants rushed about, arranging flowers and streamers throughout.

The butler motioned to a richly appointed room to the right of the main entrance. "Please make yourselves comfortable, gentleman."

With a nod, he disappeared down the long hallway to the rear of the manor. We waited, admiring the lavish decor and occupying ourselves with idle conversation.

Louis looked as if he had freshly awakened from a long nap, ready to take on the world, while I must have been showing a fair bit of my own self-inflicted misery. Two bottles of wine mid-day had only left me with a massive headache and a wish to find a soft place to lay down for a bit.

Well over an hour later, a wigged gentleman burst into the sitting room, dabbing at his forehead and neck with a handkerchief.

Both Louis and I leapt to our feet upon his entrance and stood casually at attention.

"M'lord," Louis said, bowing low.

I followed suit, bowing, though not as low as Louis.

"You must be Captain Louis Bochard," the man said. "You'll have to forgive my delay, sir. Today is my youngest daughter's sixteenth birthday and we are preparing for the celebration tonight," he said, dabbing at his neck. "Oh my, I forget myself. Governor Bertrand d'Ogéron, at your service, gentlemen," he said with a gentle bow. "My man said that you'd mentioned the sinking of Spanish ships."

"Indeed I did, m'lord."

"Then come, let us withdraw to my office to discuss business," he said, exiting the room through a side door leading into a lavishly appointed office. Governor d'Ogéron went directly to the sideboard and poured himself a drink.

"I'm quite parched myself," he said looking back over his shoulder at us. "Would either of you care for a drink?"

"That would be wonderful," Louis said.

I politely turned down the drink, still regretting my earlier decisions at the tailor's shop.

"This, my good captain, is some of the finest whiskey that you'll find anywhere on the island. Better than any of that swill shipped in from England or Portugal. And, dare I say, better than any spirit produced in France, but I may be somewhat prejudiced." The governor smiled, handing Louis a half-filled tumbler of whiskey.

Louis held the glass high with a thankful nod then sipped.

"Delicate, yet bold with a hint of cinnamon and cardamom?"

The governor smiled proudly. "Indeed, that is it exactly." He removed his jacket, then eased himself into a high-backed leather chair, propping his feet onto a matching ottoman.

"To business, shall we? You haven't come all this way to merely sample the whiskey, and I have a soiree to prepare for. And please, do sit. I am exhausted as it is. You are making me even more tired just seeing you standing there."

"As you wish, monsieur," Louis said. He slipped into a seat across from the governor. I sat as well, but off to the side where I could easily watch the two of them at work.

"I will get straight to the point."

"Please do," d'Ogéron said, taking another sip.

"I am the captain of the *Sea Nymph*, a twenty-gun corvette which is being refitted as we speak. We are here in the hopes that we may procure a Letter of Marque against Spanish vessels sailing these waters and beyond."

"That's it?" The governor looked taken aback. "And I expected a request of the impossible." He laughed. "A Letter of Marque is a simple enough matter to attend to. I will happily draw up your license," he said, making his way over to a massive mahogany desk. "You said that your ship's name was the *Sea Nymph*, correct?"

"Aye, that I did, sir." Louis stood, making his way to stand before the governor's desk.

The governor produced a pre-drafted document from a desk drawer, then quickly dipped a quill into an inkwell and began filling out the remainder of the document, signing with a flourished scrawl.

"Done." He tossed the document across the desk to Louis who immediately read over the letter.

"This looks to be in good order. Thank you, monsieur."

"My pleasure," said the governor. "Now, if our business is concluded, I must get back to…"

"Father," a young girl called as she burst through the office door we had entered from. Noticing Louise and myself after her rude entrance, the girl stopped dead in her tracks, looking abashed. I quickly stood, showing my respect for the fairer of the sexes.

"Gentlemen, my daughter, Jacquotte," the governor introduced.

"I am sorry, Father. It didn't occur to me that you may be in council."

"Think nothing of it, my dear. Is there trouble?"

"No, Father. Not as such. Only a quarrel of who will be quartered near who is all. It can be dealt with later." She eyed both of us with a mischievous eye.

"And will you gentlemen be attending my party tonight?"

"Jacquotte," the governor interrupted. "They were just about to leave."

She tucked her arms behind herself and rocked on her heels. "Nonsense, Father. I insist. They must stay. A few new faces will liven up the party and the stuffy conversation that I'm sure will abound throughout the night."

The governor smiled, a look of annoyed pride dancing across his face.

"Well, gentlemen? I for one am not one to refuse a lady's request, especially

when she knows exactly what she
wants."

Chapter 7

Governor d'Ogéron called on one of his many staff and had a room arranged for each of us in the manor's guest wing. We retired to our respective rooms to freshen up and prepare ourselves for the party.

I for one washed my face in the basin of cool water supplied me, then stretched out on the massively lavish bed.

Louis on the other hand had a different definition of freshening up.

"Did you know that they have apparently supplied a bottle of the island's finest rum for each of the guest rooms in this wing," Louise said as he barged into my room.

"I did not," I said, rubbing my eyes with the heels of my palms.

"My guess is that they have supplied it as either a digestive or to combat the ill effects of insomnia that plague so many of the upper class."

Louis sat on the bed, leaning against the headboard, he propped his feet across my abdomen.

"What exactly do you think that you are doing?"

"Containing you, so that you may also enjoy the full hospitality of our gracious host," he said. A slight slur began to form at the edge of his speech. I looked up at the clinking of glass against glass to find Louis pouring rum from a beautifully etched decanter.

"Let us toast to good fortune and prosperity." He held out the partially filled glass to me as he slid his feet aside, letting them dangle from the edge of the bed.

"Are you drunk?"

Louis shook his head and smiled. "Absolutely not, my dear, Rory. We must make a good impression on these pampered ninnies if we wish to establish valid business connections among their personage. Therefore, I will not get drunk, but taking the edge off before dealing with these aristocrats never hurt anyone in even the slightest."

I sat up, taking the offered glass. "Fair enough," I said, holding my glass high. "Sláinte."

"À votre santé," Louis replied, then tipped back the decanter. He gasped for breath. "God, that is good rum."

"While I do agree," I said, taking a sip of the fragrant amber liquid, "I'll still observe a bit more temperance than that if for no other reason than the sake of my pounding head."

"Oh, do pull that stick out of your ass and try to relax for a moment, Rory." He clinked the decanter against my glass. "Bottoms up." He smiled and took another large drink from the decanter.

A number of hours later, guests began to arrive just as dishes of hors d'oeuvre were placed on tables along the back wall of the grand hall.

We dined and rubbed elbows with some of the wealthiest and most influential people on the island until the wee hours of the morning. Plantation owners, merchant captains, and several powerful businessmen from the old world were in attendance.

At one point, long into the night, I noticed Louis fanning himself, looking a bit pale before he escaped to the estate's patio. I followed a few moments later.

Several small groups and couples had moved out of the stuffy house to the much cooler patio. A steady, refreshing sea breeze wafted up from far below.

Spotting the distinctive feather from Louis's hat retreating down the stairs to the gardens, I followed. Moments passed as I watched him casually stroll the paved path, literally stopping to smell the roses in the bright moonlight.

"Louis," I said softly, announcing my presence. He turned, looking to me with a wide smile that crossed his face. "Are you alright?"

"Oh, more than alright, my boy."

"You looked ill when you left the party within."

"While true that the fumes had almost consumed me within, a refreshing stroll and a breath of something beautiful have all but restored my previous constitution."

He bent once more, taking in another deep breath of the closed flowers. "It truly is the small things in life that matter the most, Rory. And if you don't slow down from time to time to stop and smell the roses," he said with a sideways nod toward the flowers, "the finer things in life may pass you by, never to be experienced and enjoyed."

"And I take it that this is one of those moments?"

"Precisely." He smiled and stepped closer. "I fear that I am not quite ready yet to return to the party within, but a stroll throughout the garden may just be the medicine to cure what ails me." He raised his elbow, offering me his arm as an escort. "Care to take a stroll with an old skallywag through a moonlit garden?"

"I would," I said. Taking the captain's offered arm, we leisurely set off for the nearby entrance to the estates' gardens.

We strolled in complete silence for a long while, enjoying the pleasant scents of fragrant flowers, and beautiful star-filled canopy overhead.

Several others in attendance at the party had escaped to the gardens as well. Whether for the fresh air or for a bit more privacy, we did not stop to ask, though the latter was quite apparent with many of the couples hidden about alcoves along the garden path.

Arriving at a small, rose-covered gazebo, we climbed the steps and took a seat on a stone bench. For a few, completely silent moments we watched the waves lap at the beach far below at the base of the hillside.

A joyful smile painted Louis's face with warm, happy lines as he stared off into the starry distance.

"A penny for your thoughts," I softly probed, "even though you look quite happy and content, something still weighs upon you."

He let out a laughing snort then turned his smiling countenance toward me. "I am, my dear Rory. I am." He patted my knee, resting his hand atop mine. "And at the same moment, you are correct. Something does weigh on me, quite heavily I might add."

"Has something happened over the course of the evening that I was not witness to? There were very few times we have been a part of separate conversations this night."

"No, my dear, Rory. Nothing like that." He stared off into the distance, drifting off in thought once more. His smile twisting slightly into a look of serious contemplation.

"Neptune has blessed me, *mon cher garçon doux.*"

A tear formed at the corner of his eye.

"I have been more fortunate than most. After many years of struggle and hard work with a little help from lady luck, I have a mighty ship and a strong crew."

"So this," I said, wiping away the tear that threatened to drop, "is a tear of joy?"

He sniffled and turned away. "I wish it were that easy."

"Then what is it, Louis? I'm sure that something can be done to cure what ails you."

He laughed, letting out a long frustrated sigh. "*Pour l'amour de tout ce qui est saint, tu es un innocent, n'est-ce pas?*" He turned back to me and shook his head.

"You are a good and loyal man, Rory. People love you, and one day many men will follow you. But we each have our own path to blaze in this world." He wiped at a sniffle that threatened to escape his nose. "You, young Rory, are as free as any other member of the crew. You may take your leave at any time from the ship's rosters as with any other man aboard. I have very much appreciated your help this day and your company this evening. It has been refreshing to be as candid as we have been these last days."

Tears welled up once again at the corners of his eyes, threatening to escape. "Be sure of the life that you want to live, Rory. Do it on your own terms, but be content with where it may lead you," he said, gently pressing his palm against the side of my face with his other hand. "While exciting and prosperous at times, the life of a pirate is an arduous and lonely trade."

His tears broke free of their bonds and raced away down his cheeks in free-flowing waves. I have no doubt that the excess of drink had helped to loosen his well-maintained self-control, allowing his true emotional disposition to run ramshot and escape through the heavy haze of alcoholic fumes.

His hand carried the feverish heat of emotion that even in the warm Caribbean evening warmed my cheek where he'd placed it. My vision blurred, and tears began to form in my own eyes. I placed my hand over his and smiled.

Could he really be as damaged as I was? Was he a discarded nothing muddling their way through a cruel and uncaring world? Same as me…?

I stared into his bright glistening eyes. The alcohol really had released him. He wore his pain outright. At that moment his defenses were all but nonexistent, leaving him weak and vulnerable.

The eyes truly were the windows to the soul.

"I believe that I am quite content in my choice of trade at the moment, Louis."

His smile grew wider than any other I'd ever witnessed. He sobbed. The last of his psychogenic defenses broken free, allowing a tsunami of alcohol-fused emotion to wash over him.

I could feel every lonesome ebb and flow of emotion that raced through him. The lack of companionship and trust was an all too familiar landscape that I had navigated since I was young. I could feel his very soul in that moment. The enamored warmth of connection rippled over me in waves.

Placing my hand gently against his tear-soaked cheek, I leaned in closer, my forehead against his. "You can rest assured, I am secure in your friendship and confidence, Louis. I have no plans of collecting my pay and jumping ship any time soon."

Chapter 8

The late morning sun shone through the windows of the bedchamber when I awoke, Louis slept calmly, snuggled in close, his face tucked under my chin. We'd spent what remained of the night wrapped in each other's arms while Louis expelled the sum of his existence to me. Once I'd gotten him back to the relative safety of his chamber, the real tears began to flow.

I'd held him, slowly stroking the back of his sweat-soaked hair while he poured out his heart to me, for what I expected was the first time he'd ever let down his defenses and become as helpless as a newborn babe. At some point near on to dawn, he'd passed out from exhaustion, or possibly the excess of drink, and we merely snoozed until midday.

We remained until the late afternoon, talking of this and that, childhood experiences, the most delicious piece of bread we'd ever stolen. We talked, and nothing more. We enjoyed the quiet warmth of each other's company before venturing out in search of sustenance.

"Eggs sound wonderful this morning," Louis happily stated as he rolled over and stretched. "I would think that a manor as wonderful as this would have eggs available for famished guests after a long night of revelry."

"I wouldn't know," I said, rolling over onto my side. I propped my head in my hand and watched Louis twirl his mustache back into place. "This has been the first manor house I've ever had the privilege to visit."

"Really," he said, surprised and looked over at me. "Then I must apologize for my lapse in mental faculties ruining the experience for you."

"I don't believe that for one moment."

"Then how would you classify my previous disability?"

I thought for a moment for the proper word before I turned back to him. "You were overwhelmed, nothing more."

"Well, whatever you'd like to call it, I'm sorry that you had to bear witness to it." He rolled to his side, facing me.

"Nonsense. We aren't that different, you and I. Similar childhoods, similar experiences, you've only acquired more of them than I up to this point. I'm honored to have been there for you in your time of need."

"More like my moment of incapacitation."

"Stop that. There is no sense in berating yourself over nothing."

"In my experience, even the slightest lapse of control can be detrimental. Though I am much happier that you were present than any others of the crew. If anyone other than you had witnessed my, moment, I could spell the beginning of the end. The crew talk. If word were to make it to any of their ears from the guests or servants present last eve would put doubt in their minds of my ability to captain the ship and crew. Crews, especially of the privateer variety, can be volatile and fickle at best." Tiny glistenings of tears threatened at the corners of his eyes.

I scootched closer, resting my hand on the side of his face, wiping away the offending tear with the edge of my thumb. "Your secret is safe with me, Louis. And in the grand scheme, you are an unknown at the moment. Not one that these pompous aristocrats will likely remember who you were any more than what they had for breakfast two days past."

"I can only pray that you are correct and we do not have a mutiny on our hands before we can make it out of port."

"I am, I'm sure of it. Now let's go find some of those wonderful eggs you promised me."

Louise angled even closer, placing his forehead against mine. "Thank you, Rory. It has been so long since I was able to be honest with anyone." He nuzzled his nose against mine. A loose hair of his waxed mustache tickled my nose and he pressed his lips against mine. I drank deeply of Louis for a moment that felt so long as if time itself had ceased to exist.

To our surprise, the carriage driver that had brought us to the governor's estate had remained through the night, procuring himself a bit of drink and snack when the serving staff weren't looking while he waited. He even went so far as to regale us with his own adventure on the trip back. According to the driver, two buxom and high-spirited kitchen wenches from the governor's estate had lured him into their trap, restraining him for most of the night.

After returning to the *Sea Nymph,* Louis and I freshened up before he sent me to gather the ranking officers, Mister Smyth and Mister Curtis, to his quarters.

"What of our status, gentlemen," Louis asked as the pair of quartermasters entered the room.

Mister Smyth cleared his throat and answered. "The *Sea Nymph* will need a few more days to prepare to make the modifications you requested, sir. Shouldn't be a problem though. She be ready to sail now if you are so inclined. We've transferred supplies, extra guns, and shot from the *Wrath* and the *Glory*, but we haven't added the extra gun ports."

"And what of the *Wrath* and the *Glory*?"

"Sold, sir," Mister Curtis answered. "For a fine price, I might also add. Especially considering the condition the *Glory* is in."

"And how many of the crew have decided to take their leave of our rosters?"

Both of the quartermasters rocked in place, nervous glances passing between the two of them as if they were having a telepathic conversation that the rest of us could hear.

Mister Smyth began to open his mouth, only to be cut off by Mister Curtis. "Only about a quarter have taken their leave, sir."

"Those also, happen to be mostly from the slave cargo taken from the *Glory*, sir," Mister Smyth added.

Louis looked up at the pair of quartermasters, perplexed at their strange behavior. "Why do I feel that you aren't telling me everything that has transpired since my departure yestermorn?"

"Well, sir," Smyth began.

Curtis broke in, taking over the conversation. "Well, you see sir, a number of the men were on liberty in town and boasted quite a bit about how we had successfully captured the *Sea Nymph*. Apparently, there were several sailors in one of the taverns who had previously served aboard the *Sea Nymph* under the command of her previous captain."

Louis shook his head in confusion, failing to understand the problem as much as I was. "Men dedicated to the sea do tend to serve on many ships during their time. I'm sorry gentlemen, but I fail to see what the problem is, unless most of my crew are locked in irons or in the town's stocks awaiting the noose."

"They were English, sir."

Louis looked to me and back to the pair of nervous quartermasters. His face twisted with a painfully confused look of a constipated hemorrhoid. "I still fail to comprehend the issue here," he said, standing upright. Crossing his arms, he glared at the two men.

"But…," Mister Smyth began to stutter before Mister Curtis continued for him.

"Won't they want retribution for King and Country, sir?"

Louis gaffawed. "That is possible, gentlemen. But unless they have a significant force in which to overtake us with, our ship and crew will be fine.

Aren't we still over two hundred hands strong?"

"Yes sir."

"Considering we are in a French town surrounded by French waters, I doubt that even a few small English merchant ships will pose us any sort of real threat. Now… if there isn't anything else, we can get to what I wished to discuss with you."

They both nodded, simultaneously mumbling *aye, sir.*

"Good…good," Louis said. He fumbled in his jacket pocket for a moment before retrieving a small velvet pouch. He emptied the contents into his palm and held out a beautiful silver ring to each of us. It was a heavy and solid piece of metal, decorated with gold filigree, inset fish made of gold on the sides. A beautifully carved image of a sailing ship upon a polished piece of tiger's eye had been caressed into the deep setting.

"What are these for?"

"Partially a gift, partially a symbol of rank aboard my ship," Louis answered.

"A symbol of rank, sir?" Mister Smyth asked. Confused.

"Yes, Mister Smyth. A symbol of rank. To the crew, anyone who wears one of these rings," he said as he slid one onto his own finger, "is without a doubt in command. You, Mister Smyth, I have decided shall retain the rank of quartermaster. But only because Mister Curtis retains more knowledge than you do on the subject of sailing a ship." He nodded to Mister Curtis. "If you would be so kind as to humor me, sir. I would like you to continue your service with me as the ship's Sailing Master."

"But…," I started, confused. "Why did you give me one of the rings?"

"Because, Mister Odell," he said with a side-eyed wink at me. "I'd like you to become my first mate."

I shook my head, confused. "But…Why?"

"Because I see great potential in you, and should something happen to me, I need someone who the crew respects and can step into the position at a moment's notice. On the whole, Mister Smyth will be in command of most things, regardless of who the captain is. But that's just what the quartermaster does. Otherwise, you will train under me to one day captain your own ship, should you be lucky enough and willing."

I really didn't know what to say to that. There was no doubt that some level of favoritism was involved in his decision-making process. I was more than willing to give it a go, but at some point in the future, I would assuredly be confronted by the crew about it.

"Well, Messieurs? What say you," Louis asked.

Both of the older gentlemen answered simultaneously. Enthusiastically nodding their heads, they slid the rings onto their fingers.

Louise leaned onto the chart table and looked up at me. "Well? What say you, Mister Odell?"

"Aye, Captain," I said, staring at the beautifully made ring before turning back to Louis. "Aye, sir. I accept your offer."

"Excellent!" He pounded his fist against the chart table. "Now, shall we get on with it gentleman? We've a treasure to steal."

He pulled another chart from the side pocket of the table and unrolled it onto the table, placing weights at each of the chart's corners to hold it in place.

"The treasure ship in question will make a stop here," he said, jabbing a thin finger down onto the chart, "to put in for provisions and resupply. I have it on good authority that Captain Francisco Maldonado of the *Gatito de mar* fancies a number of the locals and has put in at this small village on all of his previous return trips.

From there they rendezvous with the rest of the treasure fleet in Havana before setting out across the Atlantic. At that point, they are an invincible force, up to two dozen ships strong. So we must strike beforehand. If the timing is right, we can still arrive before they set sail for Havana.

The dark of the new moon will be both an advantage and a disadvantage to us in this endeavor. But if utilized properly, I believe it will lead us to victory."

Over the next few hours, we ran through a multitude of possibilities, relying primarily on the knowledge of the area possessed by Louis and the two older sailors. After a few hours of hard debate and a bottle of rum, we settled on a solid enough plan that we all agreed could work, and work well.

I had a good feeling that we would succeed. The scenario was almost too good to be true.

We were going to steal a treasure galleon!

Chapter 9

"Just as I had said, there she is," Louis whispered. He turned and sat. Leaning back against a large palm that lined the beach, he laced his fingers together behind his head.

He was without a doubt, right. There she was, a Spanish galleon anchored in the peaceful cove.

Deciding stealth, not brawn would be our most advantageous chance at success, we set out with a party of twenty men. Louis insisted that I accompany him on this endeavor, as well as Mister Curtis, for his skill with both cutlass and pistol. Mister Smyth and the rest of the crew remained with the *Sea Nymph* to await our return, and were under orders to sail on should they not hear from us in three days.

We'd trekked through the jungle from the southern end of the island in the near pitch-black darkness. Our raiding party left out well after midnight to give the Spanish crew time to dive deep into their cups before we arrived.

Being leagues outside of the normal shipping lanes meant that they shouldn't be expecting anyone and we hoped their guard would be down even more than normal, making it that much easier to capture the prize.

"She's there just like you said, Captain." I squinted, trying to judge the distance to the galleon. Lanterns mounted fore and aft marked her location, and gave us a rough idea of how big she was. Riding low in the water, I had no doubt that her hold was full of gold and silver bullion, bound for the treasury of King Philip of Spain.

On the other side of the cove sat the Spanish captain's beach camp. Several fires burned low, scattered around the encampment.

Further up the rise to the west, fires flicked and shimmered through the undergrowth of the jungle.

"What are your thoughts, gentlemen?" Louis asked me and Mister Curtis who had stepped up beside me.

Mister Curtis cleared his throat and shifted nervously. "She being there is all fine and good, sir, but how are we going to get out to her? We could have portaged one or two of our own longboats had I known what you were planning, sir."

"Not to worry, Mister Curtis. I had a plan all along. And my hunch was correct. Did you notice the lack of activity in this small hour of the morning?"

"Aye, sir. It looks as if there isn't a single sentry on duty."

"Which means there is a very good chance that no one is guarding the longboats moored along the beach." He sat up quickly and pointed at the docks.

And sure enough, he was right. By the light cast by torches along the dock, there wasn't a soul near the longboats. The beach had been all but abandoned by the Spaniards who'd come ashore.

Even in the near pitch darkness, I could see the gleam of teeth from the men when they realized the truth of what Louis was saying.

"Then that settles it," Louis excitedly whispered. "Let's hurry to the longboats and make for the galleon. Eliminate any opposition you may encounter, but for the love of God, do it as quietly as possible." He pointed at several of the nearby men who nodded acknowledgment of his words. "Once our cover is blown, we will be overwhelmed in mere moments. Remember that."

And with that, Louis rushed forward through the underbrush, crouched low as to limit the possibility of detection. Like the thieves in the night that we were, we followed close behind the captain. If we did encounter any Spanish opposition, we could quickly and easily overwhelm any individual or even several individuals. The likelihood of encountering more than a few individuals at this early hour was highly unlikely. After my own survey of the village, I agreed wholeheartedly with Louis. By this point, the Spaniards were most likely in deep slumber after a long night of carousing and drinking.

We hurried forward, passing beyond the tree line, and in moments we were among the huts gathered around the beach side of the small dock. Louis pressed forward, turning left around what looked like a longhouse, then a right, rounding the end of the structure.

I heard the strained grunt and muffled scream before I turned the corner to witness Louis's cutlass slicing through one side of a Spanish soldier's neck. Blood spurted with each beat of the dying man's heart as he slumped to his knees, drawing Louis down with him.

That's when I noticed the dying man's hand, white-knuckled around the grip of a dagger buried to the hilt into the captain's left midsection, just below where his lower ribs should be.

"Louis!" I half shouted, and rushed forward, kicking the dying Spaniard away.

"I'm fine," Louis said, grunting through a painful cough. He waved me away and continued forward. "Don't stop. Get to the longboats."

"But you've been stabbed," I argued. He responded by pulling the blade free from his side and covering the wound with both hands, letting the blade fall away to be trampled into the sand underfoot.

"There, I'm no longer stabbed. Press on," he loudly whispered to the men, ushering them ahead of himself.

The men pressed forward, launching two of the longboats that had been left unattended on the beach. With the aid of Mister Curtis, we loaded Louis into the stern of one of the longboats near to the steersman. He slumped over, as limp as a newborn no sooner than we'd managed to push off and launch the longboat into the water.

Placing my hand over his, I almost recoiled at the wetness coating his hands and soaking his coat. It was obvious that he'd lost a lot of blood. If there were light available, I'm sure that his visage would be as pale as a freshly laundered sheet. "Louis?" I said, almost pleadingly for a response. Louis weakly coughed.

"Take the ship, Rory. The men know what to do."

I felt more than saw Mister Curtis shift uncomfortably next to me on the longboat's bench. Grabbing Mister Curtis's hand, I placed it over the captain's wound so he knew how badly the captain had been hurt.

Mister Curtis dryly swallowed. "Aye, Captain. We do."

"Good," Louis faintly coughed.

"We'll take the ship and be the richest scallywags to sail the Caribbean. You'll see," I whispered, clutching his hand in mine.

"I know you will, Rory." I felt his wet hand reach up and touch the side of my face, gently stroking at the several-day thick stubble. "Help me to sit up, my dear boy. I want to look upon our quarry."

Raising Louis from the board, I slipped behind him, propping him upright. He shook with a quiet laugh. "The crown will be livid when word finally reaches them, that a band of ruffians and scallywags overtook one of their prized treasure galleons."

I laughed as well and leaned in close to whisper into his ear. "Even more so when they find out it was a *bastard* Frenchman leading the assault."

"Indeed, *Mon… Ami.*"

He had barely gotten out the word when his hand slipped away from my cheek and his entire body relaxed against me. His last breath exhaled on those words. I held him upright there for a long moment.

I fought back a sob that welled up from deep within my chest, the pressure was paralyzing, restricting my own breathing. I'd only known him for weeks, an eternity to some, but then nothing at all to others. I'd quickly grown to admire him in recent weeks, that had become something else entirely over the last few days.

Mister Curtis must have heard the captain's release. He placed a gentle hand on my shoulder, patting it as well as any uncomfortable father figure could.

I straightened, sucking back the emotion I took a long, deep breath to center myself. Now was *not* the time to show weakness of any sort. The prize was in sight and the men needed guidance.

"We have come too far to deviate from the captain's plan in any way," I said in a low whisper to Mister Curtis. It must have been loud enough for several of the other men to hear because I could hear the sound of their uncomfortable shifting over the sound of waves lapping against the side of the longboat.

"Aye, sir. Agreed." Mister Curtis squeezed my shoulder as if to cement his decision to himself as well as me.

If Louis's soul remained within this vessel, he could continue to watch as we grew closer to our prize. I held him upright so that he could still bear witness to the results of his planning.

We continued across the dark bay, as slow and silent as an apparition. Lanterns hung from each of the three masts as well as from either end of the vessel, casting an almost ethereal glow upon the serene scene. Lady luck had to be with us. Not a soul could be seen on deck. These Spaniards had become seriously lax in their discipline. Either that or the man on watch was as worthless as teats on a boar hog.

Either way, it was to our advantage. Silently we came alongside the anchored galleon. Several of the men grabbed for the side of the ship to guide us in gently so as to not bump the longboat against the galleon's hull. Stowing their oars, the men pushed us along toward the bow and our access to the ship's deck. As men began climbing the anchor chain, I gently slipped out from behind Louis, letting him lay flat in the bottom of the longboat. Removing my own coat, I draped it over his limp form then turned back to Mister Curtis. "Ensure the longboat is tied off. The captain and the men deserve a proper burial."

"Aye, sir," Mister Curtis responded with a nod before returning his attention to the task at hand.

I could hear the sound of wet gasps from the deck of the forecastle above me before I'd completed climbing aboard the galleon. The men had found a Spanish soldier asleep on duty, resting atop several crates of cargo. They made quick and nearly silent work of dispatching him before spreading out across the main deck.

Mister Curtis led half our party below decks to begin clearing out the *vermin*.

"You two," I directed, pointing at two of the sailors who'd cleared the upper forecastle. "Raise the anchor and prepare to cast off. And you two," I said, pointing at two others, "hoist the mainsail." Each of them quietly nodded and rushed to their tasks.

I drew my own cutlass before I hurried to the door leading below into the forecastle and pushed my way into the darkness. Down the set of stairs ahead of me, I heard the scuffle of feet and the struggle of someone fighting to breathe. Reaching the bottom of the steep stairs I rounded the corner and found myself on the ship's main gun deck. A single lantern hung on a steel hook attached to one of the bulkheads about halfway down the length of the chamber. Several of our crewmen had managed to subdue and were finishing off the Spanish sailors on this level. I returned to the stairs and continued down to the next deck.

A blade flashed out from the darkness below as I found my footing at the bottom of the steps.

I ducked to the left, raising my own blade too late to deflect even a mosquito. Luckily the strike impacted the post of the stairs instead of the side of my head.

The Spaniard put his boot against the post and pulled with all of his might, freeing his blade from the seasoned wood.

"Déu lliuri tots els pirates al mateix diable," the Spaniard said under his breath as if he muttered a prayer of some sort. He stepped forward out of the shadows and into the dim light cast by the lanterns above. Guessing by his disheveled appearance and the blood-spattered across his torn shirt, he'd already encountered one of our sailors.

He lunged forward, thrusting with his saber.

Backpeddling, and stumbling over my own feet I swiped underhanded at his blade, deflecting the initial strike.

He pressed forward, thrusting with the tip of his polished blade, driving me back further into the darkness of the hold.

"Give up now and I'll go easy on you," I said, then grabbing a sack from a stacked pallet of cotton I heaved it in his general direction and scrambled to get some distance between us.

He caught the heavy bundle in his arms and stumbled back several steps. Dropping the stack to the side he sprinted forward, crossing the distance in moments. No sooner had I turned to defend myself than he planted his shoulder into my midsection, knocking me backward to the deck.

Straddling me he gripped the hilt of his blade in both hands and put all of his force into a downward thrust.

Shifting, I wriggled my head out of the way just in time. The tip of the blade impacted the wooden deck next to my head, its razor edge biting deep into the top of my right shoulder.

He rocked the blade, pulling it toward him. He leveraged it against the deck, digging it deeper into my flesh.

"Mor un gos irlandès," the Spaniard grunted through gritted teeth. Spittle flying with each forced word.

Grabbing the blade, the sharp steel bit into my hands as I fought against him. I kicked with little effect because of how he sat straddling me. He forced his weight into the blade, sliding it deeper into my shoulder regardless of how hard I pushed back against the blade.

The Spaniard let out a chuckle of laughter. "T'enviaré al diable, després pixaré al teu cadàver," he said, almost growling, then laughed again and forced the blade down farther.

I never heard the footfalls approaching, or the cocking of the hammer, but the sound of the pistol firing was all too familiar. The Spaniard's face contorted after the blossom of red that formed on his forehead and blood began to trickle down his face.

He went slack and I shifted, shoving him to the side, careful to direct the blade out of my shoulder and away from my head.

"This should be the last of them," Mister Curtis said as he came into view and stood over me. "Let's get you topside and get the wound looked after." He held out his hand and helped me to my feet. Making our way topside, I saw that the men had already begun securing cargo for travel. The ship's wide square sails billowed overhead, catching the wind and drawing us along out to sea. Signal lamps had been lit and placed fore and aft to alert the *Nymph* of our approach and subsequent success at capturing the galleon.

Mister Curtis directed me to sit on a stack of crates near the mainmast and tore at my shirt, exposing the wound. "We'll get you cleaned and stitched in no time, boy." I flinched at his prodding of the gash in my shoulder.

"How bad is it, really?"

"It's deep, but I've seen worse." He retrieved a flask from his pocket, removed the cork with his teeth, and poured the contents over the gash. I let out a grunted scream. It burned like someone had forced a hot poker into the wound.

"Bloody hell, man."

"Would you be preferring a little pain now, or the fever by morning?" Mister Curtis shrugged, then took a long gulp from the flask himself before handing it to me. "We'll find some twine and needles and get this sewn up as quickly as we can."

That's when I noticed several of the men hoisting Louis's draped figure onto the main deck with the use of a plank and sailcloth. It would be good for the men who were his loyal supporters to have their chance to pay their respects. I took another drink from the flask and turned back to Mister Curtis.

"How many more men besides the captain did we lose?"

Mister Curtis grunted a chuckle under his breath. "The captain did well in choosing you as first mate. Straight to business." He smiled and sat on the crate next to me. "Five others. All good seamen, even if they were black-hearted scoundrels. We've enough hands to sail our prize without too much trouble as long as the seas are calm and the winds are favorable."

"Good." I settled back and tried to relax my shoulder a bit. "Then if all goes well, we'll be reunited with the *Nymph* by morning and we can decide on our next step from there."

Epilogue

"He's not a sailor," McCreed, one of the ship's bosuns shouted, jabbing their finger in my direction. "He's no right to anything now that the captain has gone to visit with Old Hob."

"He," Mister Smyth shouted, pointing in my direction, "has all the rights of the first officer of this vessel, which places him in charge until a duly appointed replacement can be decided on by you lot, with myself and Mister Curtis having the majority votes in the matter." The gathering of men across the main deck of the *Nymph* shifted uncomfortably.

Two men stepped forward, blades drawn as if they were about to force a mutiny on the spot. McCreedy held his arm out in front of the other two, halting their advance. "You see that I'm not the only one who disagrees with the captain's previous decision." He turned his glare back to Mister Smyth and myself. "Upon the captain's corpse and under the eyes of the almighty himself, new leadership needs be decided before anything else."

"And who, pray tell, do you back for the captaincy?"

McCreedy flashed a wide conniving smile. "Why, myself of course, with the blessing of several of my men."

Mister Smyth climbed the aft stairs to the upper deck and turned to address the crew followed closely behind by Mister Curtis. "Captain Louis Bouchard," Mister Smyth said, motioning to the bound, blood-stained sailcloth resting near the mainmast. "Met his demise at the hands of a Spanish soldier, but continued to lead us until his earthly shell failed him. As you know, he appointed myself as quartermaster, and Mister Curtis as sailing master of the *Nymph* prior to his passing, as well as appointing young Mister Odell as his first mate." Mister Smyth held his closed fist out, showing off the ring that Louis had given him.

"Appointed by the captain, by the witness of the all mighty, and recognized by these rings as symbols of our station."

"It still doesn't change the fact that the first mate is nothing more than a doxy'd cabin boy dressed up to be something he isn't," McCreedy shouted, interrupting.

"That boy," Mister Curtis shouted, gathering the crew's attention, "continued leading the boarding party. He may not know much about seamanship yet, but he has heart. The men listen to him without question, and he's a set of balls about him that I doubt many of you might have. Yes, I had to save Mister Odell from the grip of the reaper, but haven't we all been in situations where a comrade has had to come to your aid?"

"Balls he might have, but he still isn't a sailor," another man shouted.

"He can be taught to be a sailor, or not." Mister Smyth shrugged. "He might be better suited to diplomacy and negotiations, which could very well be to our benefit and line our pockets with even more gold and silver than before. He had the faith of the captain, and you all backed *him* knowing little of him at the time."

"Not all of us backed him," McCreedy added.

"Even so. we'll stick to the original plan the captain had set in place. We sail for Tortuga, collect our bounty from the governor, and sell the galleon to the highest bidder before dividing the plunder. And we'll decide from there where to go next. So, what say you lads? Mister Odell can be taught what he needs to know, but he's a natural leader if ever I've seen one. For now, do we give him a chance or nay?"

The gathered crowd shifted uncomfortably again.

"Those in favor of Mister Odell to captain the *Nymph*, step to the port side of mainmast. Those against, to the starboard side." After some indecision and shuffling about, over two-thirds of the crew made their way to the port side of the ship. Mister Smyth and Mister Curtis both turned to me and smiled. "There you have it, *Captain*," Mister Smyth happily said. "What are your orders, sir?"

"What are you lazy assed scallywags standing around for? We've business to conclude in Tortuga. Get us underway Mister Curtis!"

"Aye, sir!"

Mister Smyth motioned for me to follow and led me into the captain's cabin, securing the door behind me.

"Thank y...," I began before Mister Smyth cut me off.

"You'll be thanking me if you make it to Tortuga with your life intact."

I shook my head, unsure of his meaning. "I thought you were backing me for the captaincy?"

"Oh, I am. But for no other reason than to keep McCreedy in check for the moment. What I need you to do, *Captain*, is to decide what it is in this world that you want. Aye, I agree with

Captain Bouchard's assessment of you, and I do believe that you will make a great leader. But between here and Tortuga, you are at risk of mutiny and death by McCreedy's hand. You'll have my full support as well as most of the crew. I'd already discussed this with Mister Curtis shortly after your return and he as well as his sailors are on board with us."

"Okay… That doesn't seem to be so much of an issue. I can avoid McCreedy and his men."

Mister Smyth laughed. "I wish it were that simple. But know that the next seven days will most likely be the longest you've ever lived. Be on your guard at all times, and you may just survive to see port once again."

We hope that you enjoyed this title and look forward to many more to come. Please, leave us a review! Reviews matter to all of our authors.

Take a look at some of our other award-winning series at https://threeravenspublishing.com/series-universes/

Visit us at https://www.threeravenspublishing.com and sign up for our newsletter for the latest and greatest news on upcoming titles and events.

Other series and titles you might enjoy.

L.N.Hunter
The
FEATHER
and the LAMP

JOINT TASK FORCE 13
AMAZON
HOLDING THE LINE
BETWEEN HEAVEN AND HELL
13

B.E.N.T.
BIOLOGIC   ENHANCED   NASCENT   TALENT

THE RAVEN
AND
THE CROW
FIND ME
ON AMAZON
MICHAEL K. FALCIANI

STARFLIGHT

You can also keep up to date with our latest release announcements on Scifi.radio and get some of the best fandom programing on the planet.

Scifi for your Wifi

And don't forget to check out the latest edition of ***Car Wars***

http://www.sjgames.com/car-wars/

Or the other amazing titles from Steve Jackson Games

http://www.sjgames.com

…or the latest in the Car Warriors:
Autoduel Chronicle fiction series.
https://threeravenspublishing.com/car-
warriors-autoduel-chronicles/